MO AND JO
FIGHTING TOGETHER FOREVER

A TOON BOOK BY

JAY LYNCH & DEAN HASPIEL

AN IMPRINT OF CANDLEWICK PRESS

A JUNIOR LIBRARY GUILD SELECTION

For Mom and Dad

–Dean

For Tristan and Seamus

–Jay

Editorial Director: FRANÇOISE MOULY
Advisor: ART SPIEGELMAN

Book Design: FRANÇOISE MOULY & JONATHAN BENNETT

 Printed in Singapore by Tien Wah Press (Pte.) Ltd.
Hardcover Library of Congress Control Number: 2007943850 ISBN: 978-0-9799238-5-2 (hardcover)

ISBN: 978-1-935179-37-5 (paperback)

13 14 15 16 17 18 TWP 10 9 8 7 6 5 4 3 2 1

WWW.TOON-BOOKS.COM

CHAPTER ONE:

FIGHTING...

GASP!
HA, HA, HA!
Let go, Saw-Jaw...
...or I, the **MIGHTY MOJO,** will punish you!

My turn to be MOJO!
No way!
MoJo
THE MI
MoJo
Way! I'll get us to the next level.
Let go, Mona! I'm about to fight Saw-Jaw!
THE MIGHTY MOJO
THE MIGHTY
KNOCK KNOCK
Someone's at the door!

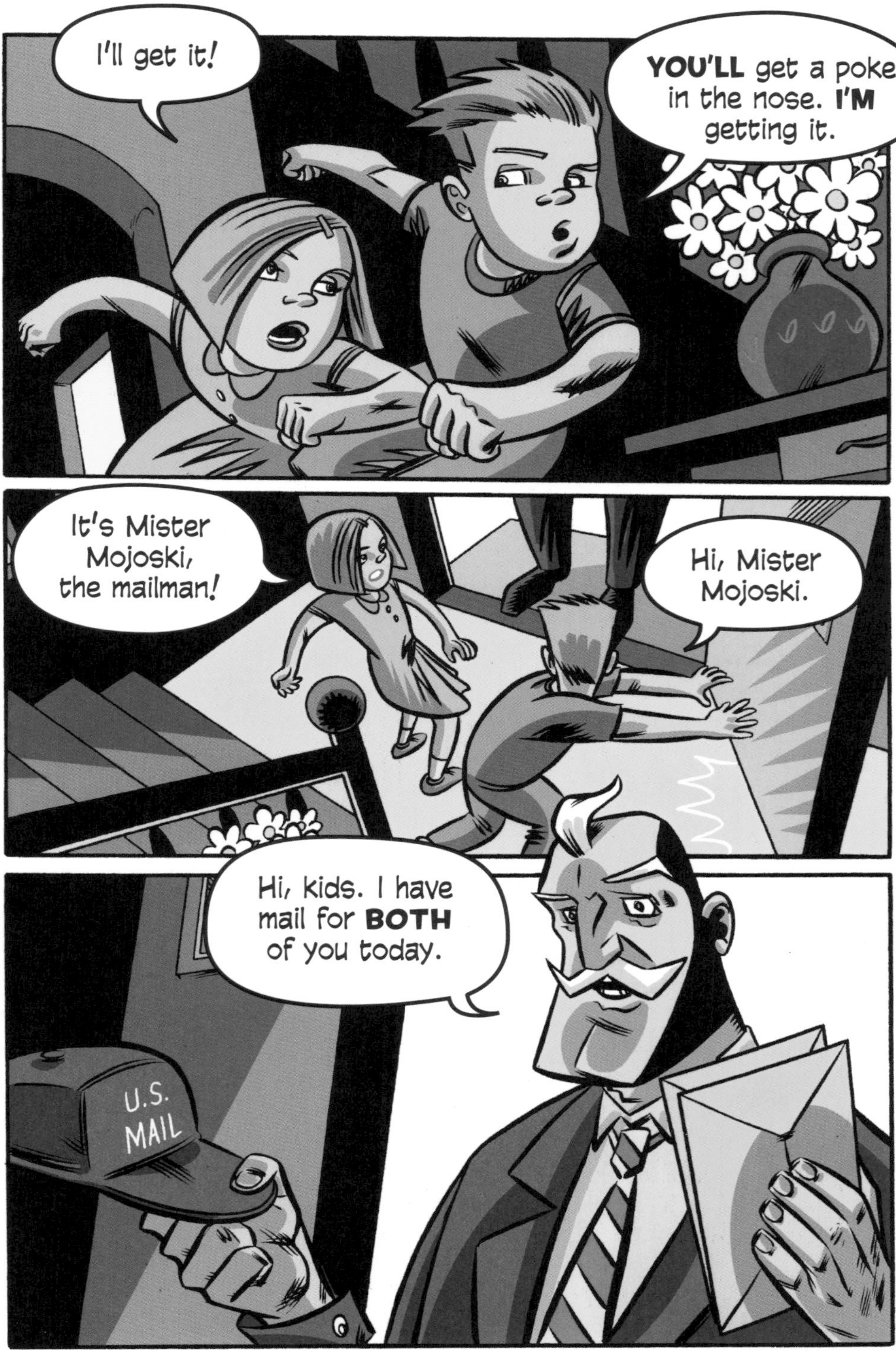

I'll get it!

YOU'LL get a poke in the nose. **I'M** getting it.

It's Mister Mojoski, the mailman!

Hi, Mister Mojoski.

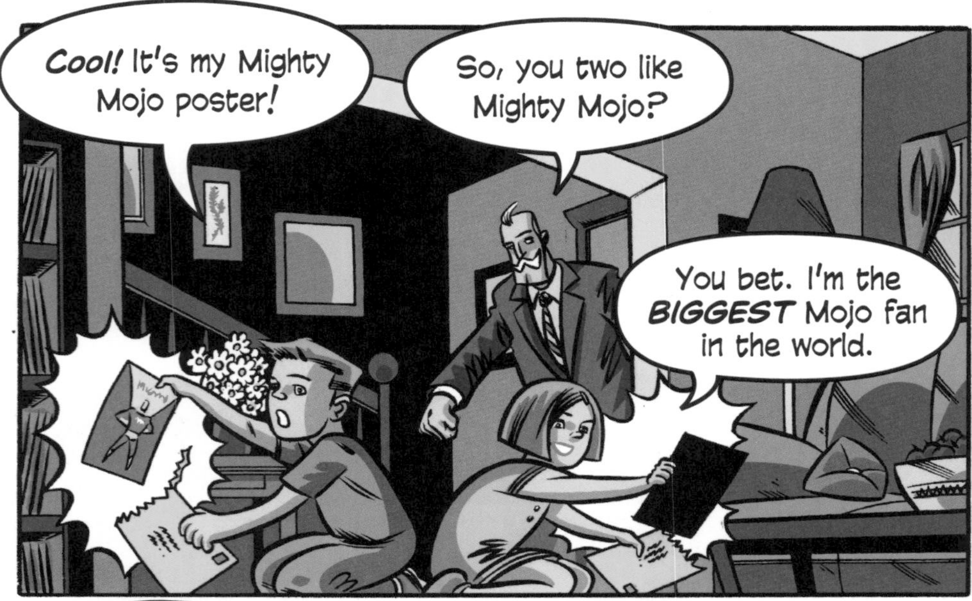
Cool! It's my Mighty Mojo poster!
So, you two like Mighty Mojo?
You bet. I'm the BIGGEST Mojo fan in the world.

No, I am!
You're the biggest PAIN in the world!
MIGHTY
MOJO
MIGHTY
MOJO

STOP! You kids are now old enough to know my secret.
MOJO

Alas, I've gotten too old for this job.

I **WAS** until today.
I'm retiring to Miami.

Maybe one of you
kids can take over
crime-fighting for me.

MOJO

HAND OVER that costume! It's MINE!
No, YOU let go! It's MINE!
MOJO
UMPH!
UMPH!
RIPPP
Now see what YOU have done? All the powers were in the costume...
...and YOU have ripped it in half!
MO
JO

Are you two fighting **AGAIN?!**
MoJo

Can't you ever **SHARE?!**

Mona tore my Mojo costume in half, Ma!
NO, ***JOEY*** did it! And it's **MY** costume!

There's a parade downtown tomorrow. I'll fix this so one of you can wear it.

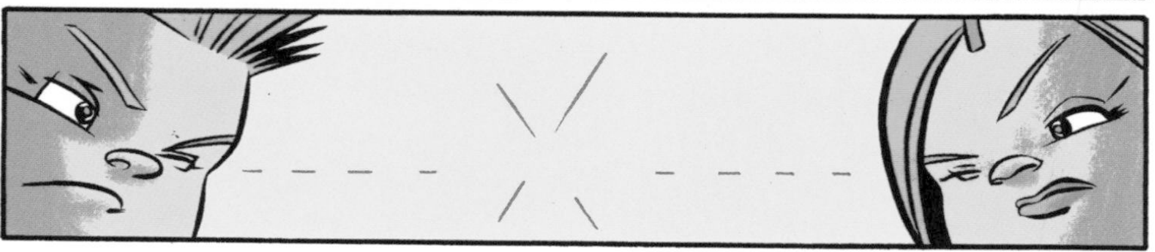

Zzz...
MoJo
Zzz...

Good morning, kids. Look, I turned it into *TWO* costumes!
?
?
MoJo
MO

One for *YOU*, Mo.
Nice!
MO
And one for *YOU*, Jo.
Cool!
JO

NO FAIR! I want the **MAGNETIC** boots.
Stop moaning, Mo. It's time for *Jo* to *GO, GO, GO!*

CHAPTER TWO:

FIGHTING FOREVER...

I'll race you to the parade. Those heavy boots will just slow you down.
HA! **YOU** slow me down, Sis! Eat my dust!
Hey, **LOOK!** I have Mojo's stretchy arms!
THAT is *BY FAR* his coolest power!
BAH! You just have the power to **BUG** me!
MO
JO
MO
JO
MO
JO

Watch what these **MAGNETIC** boots can do.
HA! What do you say to **THAT?**
I say...
...you're just a big refrigerator magnet.
And **YOU** just *stretch* my patience!
CRUNCH!

I can climb up a skyscraper just like Mojo did.
Who cares... So what!
I can reach the roof of a house just by lifting my finger!
MO
But YOU can't stop a crook by wiggling your toe!
JO
CLANK!

Stretching arms are the most important Mojo power of all!
No! Magnetic boots are better.
ARMS!
BOOTS!
I can stretch, and THAT'S the better half of Mojo.
THAT'S a stretch, and YOU are just a half-wit.
MO

The giant **HIPPO** balloon has gotten ***LOOSE!***

It's the star of the parade. I've got to save it!

OH NO! What's that following the balloon?

It looks like...

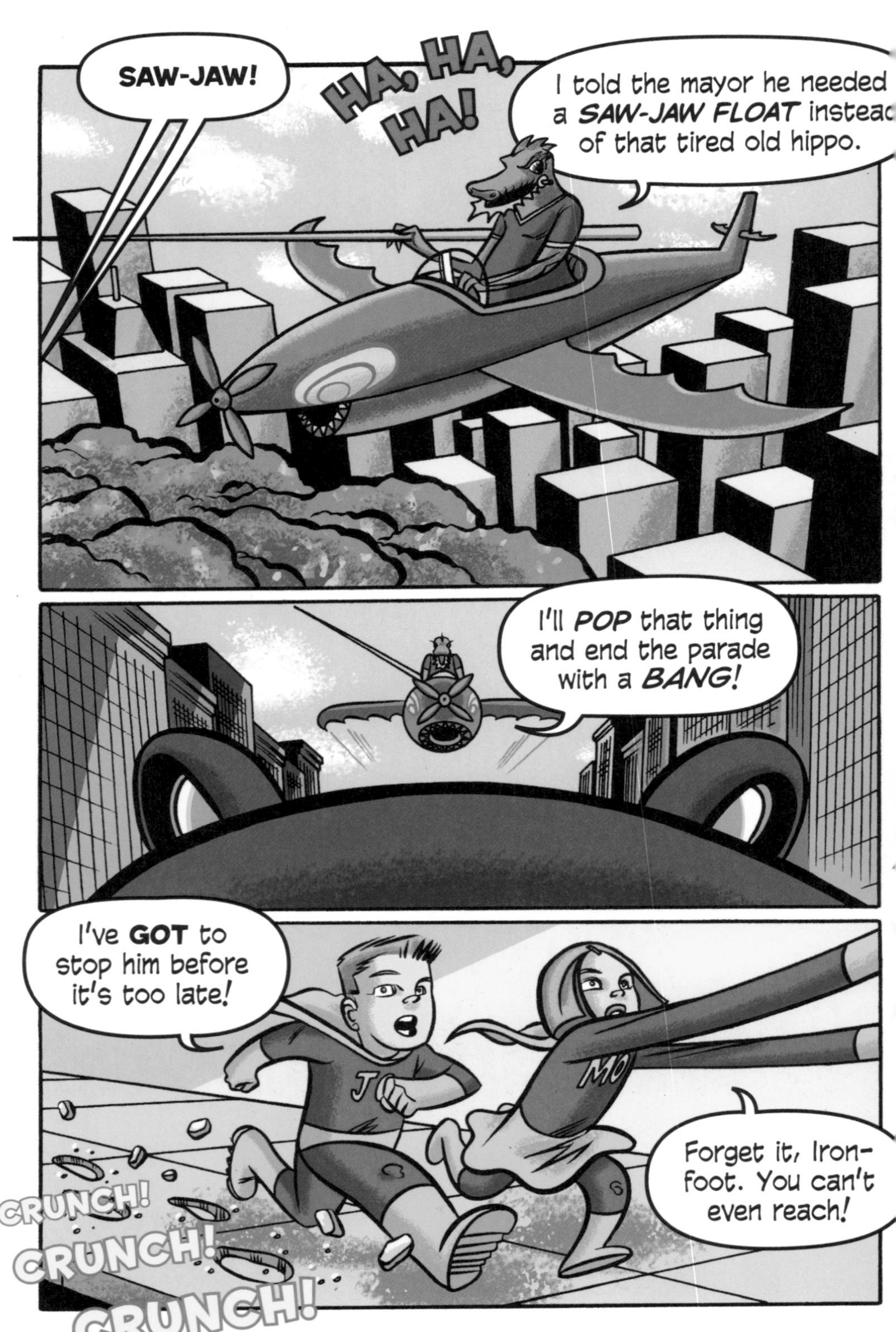
SAW-JAW!
HA, HA, HA!
I told the mayor he needed a SAW-JAW FLOAT instead of that tired old hippo.
I'll POP that thing and end the parade with a BANG!
I've GOT to stop him before it's too late!
Forget it, Iron-foot. You can't even reach!
CRUNCH!
CRUNCH!
CRUNCH!

I always wanted to **HUG** that cute hippo!
Hey, Jo! Just watch me poke a hole in Saw-Jaw's plans.
I know the costume— but I can't place the face.
I've got to get that ***GIANT PIN*** away from Saw-Jaw!
That's **MY** job! Just give me a lift!
Who needs ***YOU***? Go watch the parade, little boy!

Half my powers are in the arms of a half-wit!
Here I come...
...to fight the CROOK.
MOJO
JO
Out of the way, Mona...
MO
...you can just LOOK!
?
MOJO
JO
MO

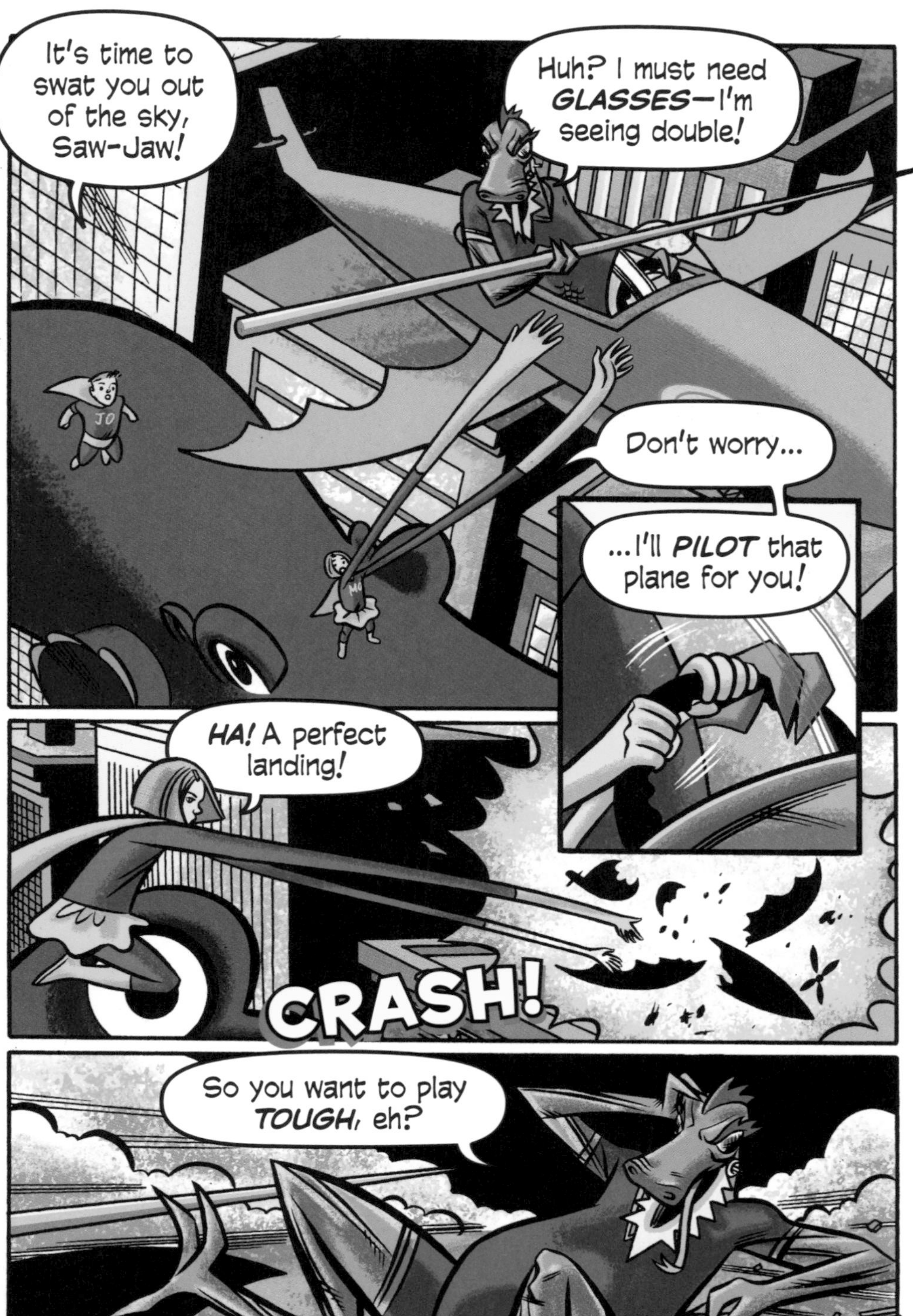
It's time to swat you out of the sky, Saw-Jaw!
Huh? I must need GLASSES—I'm seeing double!
JO
MO
Don't worry...
...I'll PILOT that plane for you!
HA! A perfect landing!
CRASH!
So you want to play TOUGH, eh?

I'm going to *POP* this balloon...
...but first I'll *PIN* these two insects!
Uh-oh!
I'll teach you to rain on my **PARADE!**
JO
Come here, my cuties. Let me give you a *TASTE* of this steel pin!
MO
STEEL pin? That gives me an idea...

Why don't I take that pin AWAY from you before somebody gets HURT!
MO
Sharp thinking, Bro!

?
OOPS!

I didn't exactly want it POINT FIRST!

WHEW! That was a close shave!

THUNK

Pins and needles...

...Needles and PINS...

YANK!

...A happy lizard is a lizard who GRINS!

Stand back, Joey!

It's time to take that toy AWAY once and for all!
?

UMPH!

WHEE! Thanks for the free ride, little girl!

You didn't get the point...
You were supposed to let go!
HA!

...Not only did I get the point, I still have the **POINTER!**
There **MUST** be some way **I** can stop him!
OH, NO!
There **HAS** to be some way **I** can stop him!
Stay out of it, monkey-brain!
Out of my way, Iron-foot!
Ha! Ha! You kids are too busy trying to stop each other to ever stop me.
♪ **POP** *goes the hippo!* ♫

CHAPTER THREE:

FIGHTING TOGETHER FOREVER...

I hate to say it, but old lizard-breath is right!

We've been doing this crime-fighting stuff all wrong.

We should work **TOGETHER,** not apart!

Right on! We've got to work as a ***TEAM!***

HEY, let go!
Hang on tight, Mo.
Now PULL!
POP!
We've GOT it!
AT LAST.
You kids never saw what Saw-Jaw's JAW can do. Give me back my pin, OR ELSE!
WHIRRRRR
WHIRRRRRR
WHIRRRRRR

What do you think, Mo? He wants the PIN!
I'll *LAUNCH* it...
Right! And I'll *AIM* it!
BLAST OFF!
?
WHIRRRRR
WHIRRRRR
Uh-oh!
WHIRRRRR

KLANK!
BZZZT
BZZT
Good work, Mo!
Good work, Jo!
BZZZT

Ow!

BOING!
POLICE

Great job, kids! I've been watching you all along.
That's what happens...
...when we work together as a ***TEAM!***
POLICE WAGON
MO
JO
POLICE

THAT'S IT! We'll call ourselves Team **JOMO!**

Yes, Team MOJO! You can be the heroes of the parade!

ER—I think Team **MOJO** sounds ***a lot*** better!

Gosh, Jo—the Mayor is going to give us a **MEDAL!**
MO
HOORAY FOR TEAM MOJO!
HOORAY FOR MOJO!

Gee, Mo. Can you reach it with your STRETCHY arms, or should I get it with my MAGNETIC boots?
JO
HOORAY FOR TEAM MOJO!
HA! HA! Those kids are twice the hero I ever was!

THE END

ABOUT THE AUTHORS

JAY LYNCH, who wrote Mo and Jo's story, loved to read funny superhero comics like *Plastic Man* when he was a kid. When he wasn't reading comic books, he would draw his own cartoon characters on the sidewalk in front of his house—then hide in the bushes to hear what other kids had to say about his drawings! Jay grew up to become a legendary cartoonist and has helped create many popular humor products, including *Wacky Packages* and *Garbage Pail Kids*. If he could have any superpower, he'd like to know what color something is just by touching it.

DEAN HASPIEL, who drew Mo and Jo, read *The Fantastic Four* and *Shazam!* when he was a kid. He admits that he used to fight with his brother all the time, too: "All siblings have a healthy rivalry, and so did we." Dean is an Emmy award-winning artist, the founder of the webcomic collective ACT-I-VATE.com, and the illustrator of comics collaborations with Harvey Pekar, Jonathan Ames, and Inverna Lockpez. He also draws for HBO's *Bored To Death*. If he could have any superpower, he'd like to fly, "because that would just be cool!"